Mickie Winkler

POLITICS, POLICE
AND OTHER
EARTHLING ANTICS

AUSTIN MACAULEY PUBLISHERS™

LONDON • CAMBRIDGE • NEW YORK • SHARJAH

Ordering Information:
Quantity sales: special discounts are available on quantity purchases by corporations, associations, and others. For details, contact the publisher at the address below.

Publisher's Cataloging-in-Publication data
Winkler, Mickie
Politics, Police and Other Earthling Antics

ISBN 9781645754671 (Paperback)
ISBN 9781645754688 (Hardback)
ISBN 9781645754695 (ePub e-book)

Library of Congress Control Number: 2020918135

www.austinmacauley.com/us

First Published (2020)
Austin Macauley Publishers LLC
40 Wall Street, 28th Floor
New York, NY 10005
USA

mail-usa@austinmacauley.com
+1 (646) 512576

Mickie Winkler is an alien from Planet Zalaria who delights in chronicling our antics here on Planet Earth.

She has observed earthlings watering their decorative plants. She marvels at the 40,000 state laws Americans pass each year. She wonders why cops buy expensive body cameras when all the cameras seem to fail. You can share her fascination with earthlings when you read her observations, all presented in very short pieces—short enough to share with guests.

"Zalarians were once much like earthlings," Winkler explains, "but alas, we now lack the ever-entertaining drive for power and sex, so evident among earthlings and chimpanzees." (Winkler, by the way, has no doubt that when female earthlings achieve parity with males, they too will demonstrate a drive for power and has so written in this very book.)

As an illegal alien, Winkler has zero inalienable rights. Before beaming back to Zalaria, she still needs to answer the question: is there intelligent life on Earth?

Table of Contents

The Watering of the Decorative Tree

Consternation

I overheard some friends at my house one night, saying, "Her tree looks more real than ours." Why was this innocent remark, even compliment, so upsetting? Why did it keep me awake that night?

Background

About six months ago, my husband and I decided we needed an indoor tree for decorative value and to clean the air.

We went to the nursery and picked out a leafy, oxygen-exchanging machine, which according to directions, 'would thrive in conditions of semi-light with weekly watering, at which time, the tree should be turned.' We rented a van, large enough to bring the tree home unscathed and religiously turned and watered the tree.

Investigation

The morning after our party, when the aforementioned conversation took place, I carefully studied our tree for the first time. It had a rich earthy odor, which as it happens, was not the odor of earth but the odor of rotting, watered straw. It didn't turn toward the sun because its trunk was formed around a plastic tube and the intriguing web-like filaments hanging from the leaves were, in fact, just threads.

When my husband came into the room, I said, "Please ask our neighbors *not* to water our tree, after all." (We were soon to leave on an extended trip.)

"Why?" he asked.

"Because," I said with the shaking voice of one is who uttering a repressed and shameful truth, "Our tree is a fake."

I threw on some yukky-don't-care-about clothes, drained the smelly pooled water, found the directions on *How to Care for Your Tree*, stuffed everything irreverently into my compact car, and drove back to the nursery from whence it all came.

Indignation

I sought out the customer service clerk and with controlled indignation declared, "This tree is fake."

The clerk, a young man of about 25, replied all too readily, "That's obvious. And what is the problem?"

I replied, "It was represented as being real. Look at these directions that were stuck in the…"

I wanted to use the word 'soil' but settled for 'bottom.'

He read them and laughed, "It is obvious," he used the word obvious for the second time, "Someone had just stuck these directions in it. And what would you like us to do?"

"It is obvious," I replied, "that I want you to take this tree, I mean take this thing, back. I don't deal in forgeries and I have the receipt."

He studied the receipt. "You bought this six months ago. Why didn't you bring it back sooner? We don't stock these decorative trees in the summer time. Besides," he argued, "This decorative tree smells like mildew. It's damaged. What happened?"

Mortification

My indignation was turning to mortification.

"It smells like mildew because it has rotted. It has rotted because my husband watered it. He watered it because the directions said to water it. He watered it once a week. And we didn't bring it back sooner, because we just discovered your deception."

The young clerk was stumped. Eventually, he turned on the public address intercom and summoned the store manager, "We have a lady here who has been watering a fake tree once a week for six months and wants a refund." This broadcast not only brought the manager. It brought the owner, his advertising director, and some cashiers.

To his credit, the clerk retained a serious demeanor as he retold my story to his boss and the owner and the director of advertising, the cashiers, and now, a gathering crowd of customers. "This woman and her husband," he related, "bought this decorative tree in January. It contained a set of instructions someone had inadvertently stuck in. So, following these instructions, her husband has been watering the tree every week." Studying the instructions further, the clerk turned to me and asked, "Have you been turning the tree, too?"

"Yes," I replied, trying to maintain a steady voice.

"She's been turning the tree, too," he repeated to the manager, the owner, and the ad manager, etc., all of whom were standing right there. "The straw has mildewed because it has been watered," the young clerk explained proudly to all his bosses, "which explains its putrid smell."

The owner turned to me and in a steady, slow, solicitous, undertaker kind of voice said, "I will give you a container of Fresh Scent. When you get home, I want you to put this tree outside in the sunlight, so it can dry. Then I want you to spray Fresh Scent on the base, being sure to point the nozzle down at the straw. Hold the can about six inches away. Would you like me to write these directions down?"

Instead of telling the owner what he should do to himself, I said meekly, "no," and the retinue escorted me and the smelly 'tree' and the free container of Fresh Scent to my car.

As we approached the vehicle, the ad director was overcome with an attack of creativity. "Would you be willing to do a T.V. testimonial for our fakes," she asked and eyeing my impromptu clothing whispered, "You could keep the classy outfit we'd provide."

Those Earthlings

Daddy, what are they doing?

Who? The earthlings? Oh, they're having sex. They love to have sex.

But Daddy, how can they like it? They are jumping around on the bed, sticking their tongues in each other's mouths, making werewolf moans and pig-style grunts. Yuk. Why?

Well, once upon a time they needed sex to make babies. Now, they mostly have sex for fun.

Daddy! You call that fun?

Look. The man can't undo something on that women's back and is going bonkers.

Zugo, their whole society is fueled by sex. You see those clothes, makeup, jewelry, hair styles? They are all done for sex.

You mean that guy has his head shaved for sex?

That's the style. He thinks he looks great.

And that woman is walking on shoes with nails for sex?

You got it.

You know, Zugo. We Zalarians used to be like those pathetic, small-brained, war-making, jealous, and sex-obsessed earthlings. They are like the archaeological record of us. Long before you and I were made.

No kidding, Dad.

Yes, we eliminated sex. Then all those bad things went away, and our frontal lobes grew. Alas, we still have a useless appendix and useless toes and wisdom teeth and...

Hey Daddy. Let's go play zagabo.

The Naked Cop:
A Bedtime Story

Grandma: Okay, sweetheart. It's story time. Do you have a book for Grandma to read?

Evy: Oh, Grandma, just tell me the story about the naked cop again. Please, please.

Grandma: And will you go right to sleep if I do?

Evy: I promise, Grandma.

And Grandma Begins

Grandma: Once upon a time, not very long ago, there was a cop on the police force in Menlo, Lark, right here where we live. He was visiting a nice lady in another town who had been arrested for drugs and prostitution and she was breaking the law again. "Evy, do you remember what a prostitute does?"

Evy: She does tricks.

Grandma: Yes. She turns tricks. Well, two policemen from *her* town broke into her hotel room to arrest her. She was dressed in a topless and bottomless bathing suit and had lots of money in her hand.

Evy: Who else was there, Grandma?

Grandma: A naked man. They found him in the bathroom, leaning over the toilet bowl as if he was throwing drugs down the toilet. And who was that man, Evy?

Evy (*proudly*):	He was a cop from Menlo Lark. And they didn't realize he was a cop because he was naked and wasn't wearing his pretty blue uniform, right Grandma?
Grandma:	"You are so right! In fact, they didn't know he was a cop 'til after they officially charged him with a crime and looked at his driver's license."
Evy,	Did the driver's license say that the naked man was a cop?
Grandma,	"Yes. And I found out later that the naked man was not only a cop, but he was on duty and supposed to be working when he was arrested. So, do you remember, Evy? Did our home-town cop go to jail for his crime?"
Evy,	No, Grandma.
Grandma,	Did he get fired?
Evy,	No, Grandma.
Grandma,	You're so smart. If you go to sleep now, I'll take you to meet

	that cop tomorrow. Would you like that?
Evy,	Yes. Yes. Will he still be there?
Grandma,	Yes, he will be here until he retires on full pension in 22 years because Menlo Lark can't fire him and no one else wants him. What will you ask him, Evy?
Evy,	Hmm. Let me think. I will ask him if he learned any tricks.

Thank You, Leonardo!

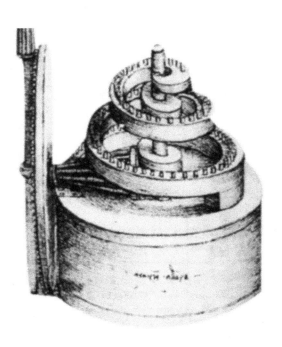

Leonardo-da- Vinci's
Invention for Opening Child-Proof Prescription Bottles

Advanced Mother-In-Lawing

Under-Handed Methods for Maintaining the Upper Hand

Who is the most reviled human being? Who is the brunt of the unkindest jokes? The title gives us away. It's the mother-in-law.

In this lecture, I will not propose that we mother-in-laws feebly protest our bad reputation. Hell, no. I say, let's get born again into society's stereotype. Let's use it to get the benefits we so obviously deserve. Above all, let's help our children expunge those feelings of guilt towards us now, while we're living, rather than suffer those unfixable feelings of guilt when we're gone.

Let's get started with my ten-point program now.

Set Goals:

Goal-setting is key. For example, the mother-in-law who wants to be fondly remembered will act very differently from the one who doesn't care what people think of her after she's dead.

Goals must be specific: A goal of 'having children love you' is vague and useless. Consider, instead, the goal of having children *demonstrate* love by, say, maintaining your car.

It's advantageous to have big maintenance goals for two reasons. First, your children will remove those daily annoyances from your life right now. And second, the more maintenance they do while you are living remotely, the less resistance they will offer when you announce that you're moving in with them.

Maximize Control: Money is always a major control factor. If you don't have money, don't despair. Just pretend you do.

Instant fortune can be achieved in several ways. If you're lazy, just claim you won the lottery. If you're adventurous, attribute your fortune to race-track or casino winnings. Assure your children you didn't tell them earlier because you're ashamed of your addiction to gambling. Guaranteed. Your children will attempt to make your life more interesting. They will not want to see you lose that fortune by gambling any more.

Will claims of making 'it big' be believable? You bet. Scientific research proves that if your kids believed in the holy gift-giver, Santa Claus, they'll believe in the promise of a big inheritance, too. You can explain your continued dowdy appearance and broken-down furniture by the age-old and effective assertion, "I don't want to be frivolous. I'm saving it all for you."

Measure Success: You'll know your strategy is working by the size of the presents you receive on your birthday and your anniversary (or anniversaries, depending on how many husbands you've had). But avoid complacency. Keep your kids alert and anxiety ridden. Which brings us to part four of the program.

Replace Guilt with Fear: We hear every day about scams practiced on unwitting elderly women. Become one. You are sure to get attention by saying, "I met the nicest man coming out of the bank. He offered to handle my financial affairs for me." When guilt no longer works, fear does, providing your kids think that your money is actually theirs.

Practice Unpredictability: Eccentric behavior becomes a 'rich,' widowed mother-in-law like yourself. Try leaving a $100 tip at a restaurant. When your kids protest, say assertively, "I liked the service." or to arouse even more alarm say, with surprise, "$100?? Oh. I thought I was leaving just $1."

My Mom Doesn't Do Things Like That. Is your child's career sensitive to public opinion? The answer is affirmative if s/he holds public office or works for a bank. In that case, it's time to dispel the arcane notion that 'my mom doesn't do things like that.' Yes, she does. And she does it in front of lots of people. She proves her command of obscene language at local town meetings. She brags about her sexual prowess on call-in shows. Not only does 'she does those things,' but she will continue to unless her children fill her needs.

Attach Strings: Take a clue from America's foreign policy: give aid, so you can take it away. Paying a percentage of the mortgage provides marvelous leverage. Or make contributions to the local symphony in the name of your children. Nobody, not even your musically illiterate offspring, wants their names removed from the prestigious playbill list.

Your sons may be pot-bellied. Your daughters may be post-menopausal. Their spouses may be sick or gone. Age is no matter. They are never too old to be bought.

Sibling Rivalry, Promote It. Remember how you used to wish your children would stop fighting? If you take this program seriously, those days are gone. Never miss the opportunity to instigate competition, not just among siblings, but among their spouses and your grandchildren as well. To the winner goes the alleged spoils.

Be Patient: There are inevitably times in the best of advanced mother-in-lawing when patience is required and you must go with the flow, like when your children claim to be in love. And this may happen all too frequently as they bumble from one marriage to the next. But be assured, their love, like the gold-plate on the chain that your late husband gave you, will eventually wear off.

Give Them Hope: You have moved in with your children. One bedroom and one bathroom in their house is now yours. You have commandeered the telephone, often by claiming that the 'doctor is about to call back.' But you notice a certain impatience setting in on their part. The last time you rummaged through their bedroom, you found the phone book opened to the 'Nursing Home' page.

Now is the time to give them hope that your demise is imminent. Cite your parents or grandparents who died young. Put your living will on the bulletin board, forbidding any major operations (but be careful, do not sign it). Complain a lot about non-descript problems. Share your wonderful dreams of heaven with them.

And Whatever Else You Do, Stay Focused on the Here and Now: If you take your mother-in-lawing seriously, you will be well attended for life. As for post-life, like after the will is read? Take advanced heart in knowing that you will always be remembered, even if not revered.

Shakespeare, I Need Help

(To Shakespeare from Susie Smith)

Dear Shakespeare,

My brother-in-law is pregnant.

As you probably guessed, he changed his gender identity from female to male before he married my sister, but after he was already expecting.

My sister is looking forward to having the child. The problem is my eighty-year-old folks. How to tell them? How to tell them that the guy my sister has married is pregnant.

Sincerely,
Susie Smith

(From William Shakespeare to Mickie Winkler)
Good Susie,

Think on these ideas.

Tell your parents not. Your sister and spouse should go hence to someplace else and re-appear after the baby is born.

Alternatively, disguise your sister to look pregnant. Rehearse her to appear sickly in the early months and to jerk as if feeling kicks, later on. During this time, hide her spouse. Your parents probably dislike him and will be glad he's somewhere hence.

However, I will, in truth, wager that your good parents already know and are mirthfully telling all their friends that—guess what? Their son-in-law is with child.

Your Faithful Servant,
Will

Being Dead Is So Damn Frustrating

There we were, in my apartment
My grown son, Carl.
His father and my ex-husband, Nathan.
My pathetic, current husband with
high-pitched whining voice.
Me, lying on the carpet, dead.

Carl, son:
The Doctor called it suicide. But why, why would she kill herself?

Ben, current husband, tentatively:
She was a little depressed.

Nathan, first husband:
You twerp. I would be depressed, too, if I were married to you.

Carl, contradicting Ben:
Actually, she was jazzed. She was just proclaimed a Life Master at bridge.

Nathan:
Lifeless Life Master, I'd say.

Carl:

Mom would not commit suicide without leaving an explanation and lots of instructions.

Nathan:

Yeah. She might relinquish life, but she sure wouldn't relinquish control.

Carl:

Well, if she didn't commit suicide, she probably got sick or ate something rotten or... Let's get an autopsy.

Ben, more forcefully:

She was really *very* depressed.

Nathan:

In the T.V. shows I watch, life insurance policies are voided by suicide, but murder still pays. Did she have life insurance?

Carl (looking in file):

I found her life insurance policy. Sure enough. Your T.V. shows are right.

Nathan:

Your mom was so money minded that she would have cashed in the policy before cashing out.

Carl:

But it says that funeral costs are covered, no matter cause of death.

Nathan:

Yes. She'd want a funeral. The rabbi would have to say something nice about her!

Ben (taking policy from Carl):

Let me see. The insurance policy names the crematorium. I will call and make arrangements.

Carl:

Not so fast, Ben. Remember the autopsy.

Carl (goes to file again):

Let me check Mom's will.

Nathan:

Please do. No doubt she left me an apology for crashing my prized Lamborghini.

Carl:

Dad, look. Look at Mom. I swear her middle finger is moving.

Carl, now looking at the will:

The will says everything goes to me. The money, paintings, furniture. Ben gets to keep his clothes.

Nathan:

I bet he'd rather have Mom's.

Carl, looking up:

Hey, there's a blank spot on the wall. Where's the Hockney?

Ben:

Oh, that was mine. Your mom bought it for me. So sweet.

Nathan:

Sweet? Sweet? She was sweet like you are smart.

Carl:

Ben, the Hockney is in her painting list and was left to me.

Ben:

Oh no. the Hockney was mine and I sold it so I could buy us a new bed—to help her back, you know.

Nathan:

Yeah, she was always bellyaching about her back.

Carl:

According to the internet that Hockney was worth $2 million, Ben. Where's the money?

Ben:

"Well, I gave the money to some friends of mine."

Carl:

Ben, for god sake, what friends?

Ben:

That's a great question. Well, some friends who said I owed them money.

Carl:

Keep talking.

Ben:

Some friends who say I still owe them money, and may come here looking for me. Not good friends. I would say big friends.

Nathan:

Can you believe? He was more scared of his big friends than he was of Mom. What a pussy she must have become.

Carl:

Ben, did you poison Mom? Fess up. How did you kill her?

Ben:

Oh, god. She had just made lasagna and I put rat poison in her portion.

Nathan:

Bet her portion tasted better than yours.

Carl:

Rat poison?

Ben:

Yes, she hoarded it. Was afraid it was going to be banned.

Nathan:

Guess those stupid animal rights folks have run out of causes and now they're protecting rats.

Carl:

That's it. Ben murdered Mom. Forget the autopsy. Call the police.

Ben:

Better tell them to get here before my friends do.

Nathan, pushing Ben out the door:

Ben. We don't want you chopped up on the carpet. Please wait for whomever comes first outside.

Carl, a few minutes later, looking out the window:

Hey, the bad guys got Ben. The police got the bad guys.

Nathan:

Except for the fact that your mom is dead, all is well.

Carl:
I guess we can call the crematorium now.

Nathan:
Let's get the jewelry off Mom first before her arms turn green. And tell those pseudo-sad folks at the crematorium to return all the gold they take from her teeth. Her teeth were her Achilles heel.

Nathan:
You know, Carl. If your mom wasn't dead and hadn't crashed the Lamborghini, I'd ask her to marry me again.

Carl
Hey, Dad. Look at Mom. I think she's sort of smiling.

Toilet Equity

We women are hopping mad that transgenders are getting the bathroom spotlight when we bone-fide females have been suffering toilet inequity since, well, God fashioned us from the rib of man.

Don't get me wrong. We welcome our gay brethren into the female fold—as long as they now join us in protesting our toilet plight and do not revert to manhood when confronted with long lines for the ladies room.

With that, let me introduce myself. I come to you today as the president of **WO-SEAT:**

> **WO**men in
> **S**upport of
> **E**qual
> **A**ccess to **T**oilets.

The inspirational start of our movement occurred way back in April of 1995, during an Elton-John concert in San Diego. Women, who were missing the concert because the lines for the ladies room were so long, invaded the almost-empty men's room to claim what they called their rightful seats. In response, one Bob Glaser filed a claim for $4.5million against the City for 'embarrassment and emotional trauma.' I'm not making this up, you know!

We did not know whether to applaud Glaser for bringing this serious issue to the attention of the world or be appalled at the possibility that a man was poised to win millions because women don't have sufficient facilities. But one thing is certain; this case was not frivolous as the court later claimed.

Men, did you ever miss a concert because you were waiting for a urinal? Of course, you didn't. But for even the most uptight women among us, it's commonplace. And we will no longer stand for it.

Do not worry. I am not recruiting toilet-equity activists. My goal today is to make you aware of WO-SEAT. It is our hope that henceforth, whenever the conversation turns to *toilets* at work, at dinner, or in church, you will speak out on behalf of our urgent cause.

So, what else is WO-SEAT doing about this gross inequality?

Well, we are *not* waiting for the Supreme Court or any other court to grant immediate relief.

Nor do we agree with those nationally-known toilet gurus who say that all restrooms should be made unisex. Of course, unisex facilities are fine for the one-seaters common in offices and small restaurants as long as men put the toilet seat up when urinating and then down when they're through.

But for large public toilets? No. To the gurus we say, "Unisex toilets would indeed be an excellent resolution if only there was only one sex. But we women do not want any dick-waving perverts stalking our restrooms. And we absolutely reject the guru's suggestion that cameras be mounted in each stall so security guards can watch and protect us."

So what are we doing? We are in action mode. In public places throughout the land, we are posting the letters 'WO' in front of the word 'MEN.'

We at WO-SEAT believe that that when all signs say '*women*,' and none say '*men*,' toilet equity will be achieved.

Grandchildless

My husband and I feel barren. I have two sons from husband number one, but neither of them has children. The only picture I have in my wallet is of me on my driver's license.

My younger son and his wife talk about having children, but only after he pays off his graduate-school debt and she finishes incurring more debt by going to graduate school. At this rate, those two will need reproductive-organ implants if they ever want kids.

As for my oldest son, he and his wife have been totally turned off to the joys of parenting by their child-obsessed, intellectually numbed, and exhausted friends.

"Ah, but what if," my husband asked my oldest son, "your child had grandparents who were like surrogate parents; available in emergencies, in the evenings, and on weekends."

"Okay. Now we're talking," my son said.

"About whom are we talking?" I asked.

"Well, if we're going to fulfill our evolutionary urge to cast ourselves into the next generation, I feel we have to help our children," my husband mused.

"Do you have an urge to be re-infected with childhood diseases?" I asked him, "Do you have an urge to get a back replacement, so you can lift a kid? Just how strong is this evolutionary urge of yours?"

"What about you?" he replied, "You could buy a new wallet with room for lots of pictures. You could get me to go to the rodeo."

"Yeah, and the dance recitals and school plays and hear kids ruining music with their violins. And their friends who put their mouths on our glass table?"

"I've got the evolutionary urge," he responded, "It overcometh reason."

"And capability. And may I remind you that you have extendeth this evolutionary urge not unto your own seed, but to my ex-husband's seed. You will be, in biological jargon, grand-cuckolded."

"When I was young, I was too impatient and self-occupied to have children," he said, "But finally, I have the wisdom and time to be a good father. I mean grandfather," he said.

At that point, my son, dense as he is, gets concerned, "I am beginning to feel like a surrogate child maker. Would I get to spend time with this child? What are my rights?"

My husband rises to eloquence, "You get to fulfill your evolutionary urge for children, as does your wife. You get the children whenever you want. You get credit for paying for everything; from karate to computer-hacking lessons and for all the many special events we take them to. Consider, these children are your ticket to grandchildren, who you can bring up in any manner you deem best."

"Yea," he went on, "Give unto me a pre-childbearing agreement, and to it will I affix my signature."

And I suspect from my daughter-in-law's super-sickly look of late that we soon will feel barren no more.

Horny Goat Weed

I first encountered Horny Goat Weed in my father's medicine chest. Horny Goat Weed? It was the only non-prescription bottle there. Before I gave Dad my self-righteous 'why are you wasting money on voodoo pills' lecture, I decided to arm myself with some facts.

I learned that Horny Goat Weed was consumed by the Yin Yang, a mythical goat-like creature admired for achieving one hundred climaxes a day and has been used for centuries in China to combat 勃起功能障碍, erectile dysfunction.

I learned that not only is Horny Goat Weed used to reverse E.D., it is used to cure weak back and knees, liver disease, aids, and much more.

What I mostly learned is that Dad had E.D. and was trying to reverse it. Go, Dad! But what about Viagra? In 1998, Viagra exploded onto the scene with one of the most convincing lines in advertising history

'If your erection lasts for more than four hours, seek emergency medical help.'

Because of Viagra, age-related sex problems became dinnertime parlance. Viagra took the shame out of a drooping dick.

But alas, Viagra is not for everyone. Viagra is specifically not for folks like my dad who can't afford a pill that costs $60 a pop. If ever the disparity between rich and poor is evident, it is between the *Viagra haves* and *Viagra have nots.*

Thanks to the demand generated by Viagra, Horny Goat Weed entered the U.S. market big time, appealing to Viagra wannabes. And guess what? Traces of the active ingredient in Viagra, Icariin, is found in many of the Horny Goat Weed brands.

My self-righteous attitude was flagging and was ultimately placed on permanent hold when I noticed that my folks were increasingly chipper-- and my father's athlete's foot was cured.

I Can't Find My Temper

Where's My Temper, Part 1

I can't find my temper. I remember leaving it with my husband, not because he banged my car with his, but because of what happened after.

Here's what happened after. Our insurance agent and neighbor advised us not to report this mishap, "If you report it, you will probably not get reimbursed because your deductible is so high, but your insurance costs will surely increase because your husband caused an accident." A great piece of logic followed by an unfortunate choice of words.

"I did not cause this accident!" husband bellowed, "She (that would be *me*) parked catawampus in the garage."

This was not heading in a good direction. We have, somehow, tripped husband's evolutionarily imbedded conviction that he does not hit a parked car. He is pounding the concrete floor with a hammer he found lying around. I am yelling, "Stop!" And the neighbors have reported domestic violence to the police.

Here come the paramedics and the police. Lots of them. Ready to cart my hammer-pounding husband to jail. I finally convince them all that I am okay. That the only victims were the cars and now the garage floor. And that he has not *yet* committed domestic abuse.

This encounter motivates husband to charge into my vegetable garden and pick vegetables, stalks and all, adding my garden to the victim list. I look for a friendly neighbor who can at least approach my husband before he rips out the peas. "Gary, go help him," I plead. Gary, slightly misinterpreting my plea, joins my husband in the garden and ferociously helps him to rip out the plants. Husband sits down and just laughs and laughs.

"Honey," he says to me, "Don't worry. I'll take care of the cars." He has found his temper in the garden. But where will I find mine?

Finding My Temper, Part 2

Don't despair, dear reader. I did find my temper. How? By chopping off my husband's dick? No. By posting his pathetic excuse for a body on the web? No.

Here's how. I held a private trial; awarded myself $30,000 for pain and suffering; this, I lifted from our joint account and re-deposited in mine. Life is good again and I feel richer for the experience.

The 'Led' Pipe

"A curse on your language," my angry Russian student yelled. He was trying to learn English. I was trying to teach it. And I had just corrected his spelling.

He had written 'led' pipe which I corrected to 'lead' pipe, which is what *led* to the frustrated outburst.

"You're making this up!" the student yelled again when I wrote on the blackboard, "The teacher *read* to her class during nap time and then asked a student to *read* out loud."

"I know it's non-sensical," I said, apologizing for my native language, "But if you just remember what you *hear here* today, *our hour* together will have been well spent."

Class finally ended on a positive note with my students pledging to win the next war, so that Russian could replace English as the Lingua Franca.

The Latest and Greatest Religion

You Are Invited to Join

Dear Everyone,

We are proud to announce a new and improved religion to match our new and enlightened age. You are invited and encouraged to join.

Test marketing reveals that this religion is so universally appealing that it has been patented. No annoying and contentious rival sects will form.

- The religion is replete with all the good stuff we have come to expect: It is incredible.
- It is enthusiastically missionary in nature; you get a commission for every convert you make.
- It forgives all our trespasses, naturally.
- It glorifies love; all kinds!
- And it provides the rewards folks want, including an active eternal life, not the boring heavenly model.

Intrigued?

In our religion, we adherents learn to love, in fact idolize ourselves, by creating perfect self-avatars. Hence the religion's name: AVATARI™.

Our avatars include what we like about ourselves and exorcise what we think is bad.

You must come to one of our gatherings to understand the life and death-enriching attributes of AVATARI™. But first, an incredibly inspiring example of what one Avatari did. He was obsessed with cleaning his nails, so he created an avatar of himself that ditched the nail-cleaning obsession. Cool? From athlete's foot to jealousy to wrinkles on your face, you too can be improved.

And with each upgrade of your avatar, you can idolize yourself more.

Please check out our website for local meetings. Free libations are always available. And you will learn how AVATARI™ can immediately and forever create a new and more marketable edition of, yes, even you.

Kepler's Books
1010 El Camino Real
Menlo Park, CA 94025
www.keplers.com
12/12/2020 12:32:55 PM
REG #: 12   CLERK #: 2   TRAN #: 143627
  1@ $10.95 9781645754671 $10.95T
POLITICS, POLICE AND OTHER EARTHLING ANT
  1@ $30.00 9781644450215 $30.00T
  JUST US AN AMERICAN CONVERSATION
  1@ $45.00 9781524763169 $45.00T
           PROMISED LAND

Sub-Total: $85.95
Tax $7.95
Total: $93.90
Tendered: MASTERCARD $93.90
XXXXXXXXXXXXX1685 mmyy   APPROVAL 07951Z
Transaction ID: MASTERCARD
Reference No: 184913
Transaction Type: Sale

       Returns accepted with receipt:
    30 days tender used or store credit
     Returns Must be saleable condition
 Travel/Test Prep/Sale/Donation Excluded.

The New Orleans *Saints*?

Just in! The New Orleans Saints football team was told to change its name.

Rumor has it that the Catholic Church is petitioning the city of New Orleans to 'please, already, drop the word *Saints* from the name of the football team.'

"You can call yourselves the New Orleans Devils," the petition asserts, "But erase our non-violent, icons of compassion and kindness from the title of your brutal team."

Saint?

If the story is true, how will the New Orleans Saints organization respond? Will it tell the church to buzz off or will it comply with the church's request? And what about the citizens of this strongly catholic city? Does their primary allegiance lie with the Church or their football team?

This reporter has also learned that the city itself may have to consider a name change when word gets out that the Duke of New Orleans, for whom the city is named, admitted to having four illegitimate children. What, we wonder, will the new New Orleans be called?

To Hell with Vegetables!

I used to be a vegetarian. "Be green. Eat green," I said back then.

Back then, I decided to be food self-sufficient. I invested $200 in a veggie garden; from which I harvested exactly one pea pod and from which I learned how devious and fussy vegetables are. Vegetables. They demand the right kind of soil, the right exposure to sun, the right amount of water, a temperature that is just so. They are just too damn picky. And feel no urge at all to get born.

Even back then, I had rejected the upper-class veggies; the organics. No pesticides or genetically modified seeds for these la-dee-da types distinguished by the bugs that come with them and of course, their outrageous expense. If the world converted to organic farming, guess what? There wouldn't be enough food to go around.

Anyway, I didn't mean to impugn the stupid organic food fad. I just wanted to vent my veggie frustration. These days, I say, "Vegetarians are what they eat—vegetables."

Failed Vegetarian

Because I Bought a Gun

There once was a squirrel that uprooted the veggie plants on my patio. To protect my property and to reinforce my belief that we all should be food self-sufficient, I bought me a B.B. gun.

I made a target to learn how to use the thing and posted the target on the patio fence. My first shot hit the bull's eye, wow. But the B.B. ricocheted and shattered my triple-paned picture window; triple paned to reduce my carbon emissions, of course.

Then a burglar entered my house and when my new, solar-powered alarm system failed to activate, I grabbed my B.B. gun and did what any property owner has the right to do, I took aim at the burglar. Did I say "stop or I'll shoot," like they do in the movies? No, I was much too scared to speak. I just shot. And a B.B. slowly dribbled out of my gun because, as I discovered right there and then, B.B. guns need to be re-charged. The burglar laughed and left with my laptop.

I was now one angry woman. So, I bought me a real gun from a neighborhood thug. He gave me bullets, showed me how to care for it, and what to say if any of his friends broke into my house.

He told me that instead of using triple-pained windows, which as he said are expensive and 'tend to get shot out,' I could apply a transparent film to a single pane window that had the same effect. He had installed film on his 'recently acquired truck.'

He also offered me space in the backyard garden he rented on the condition I grow only organic. The planting area was caged to keep out squirrels. And he was growing flowers 'to benefit the bees.'

What did he do for a living? "I sell things," he said, "If you ever need 'anything,' I can get it for you, cheaper than Amazon, I swear, but maybe not brand new."

Several weeks later, my new friend gets arrested. I learned about his arrest when the police called. Armed with the secret knowledge that I possessed an unregistered gun, he had promised the police that I would post his bail.

He told me that he had been caught on tape 'restocking his inventory,' apologized in advance for the fact that bail was a sunk cost, but, but before he disappeared, assured me that his rent was paid, so I could use the garden 'til the end of the month.'

Economy Class Crunch

It is terrible to have long legs when flying in the confines of an economy-class seat. Being far sighted and having to hold your book far in front of you is also a handicap.

My husband and I suffer the twin maladies of having long legs and long vision, yet we balk at buying business-class seats. "Why buy seats in business class which cost $8000," we wonder, "When we can buy three economy seats for the two of us for $2000 tops."

This brilliant 'buy-three-seats-for-two-people' scheme was temporarily interrupted by two events. The first occurred when the then stewardess (now called 'flight attendant') reported our 3rd seat as 'empty' to the desk and the desk, in response, sent a standby pregnant woman to claim it. When we explained to her that the seat was ours and paid for by us, she started wailing, wailing! And my wimpy husband gave in.

So there we were, having paid for what was to be an empty seat but is instead occupied by a very pregnant woman. Just as we have long legs with no place to put them, and just as we are far sighted and unable to stretch our arms far enough to read, her condition impedes her from pulling down the tray table. So we had to share our tray tables with her.

The second event that temporally ended our buy-three-seats-for-two-people routine was 9/11. Following that awful incident, the airlines said that no baggage could be assigned to an empty seat and our insistence that the empty seat was baggage free was dismissed. Before 9/11, we were considered hard hearted and selfish. Now, we were treated as terrorists.

What to do? Should we buy a seat for our dog and carry him caged? No, especially because our dog snores. We tried buying a seat for a smallish violin and found that a violin, under duress from desperate standbys, can be considered stowable and its seat can be commandeered.

So we now buy a seat for a cello and carry the damn thing. Inexplicably, on some airlines, the flight attendant refuses to feed it. Okay, so the food is yukky and the cello doesn't mind, but the cello really wants its free drinks. And the cello also wants frequent flyer miles, which most airlines refuse to award. Can you stuff the cello case with clothes to ostensibly cushion the cello? The very short answer is 'no.' And the reason is 'because.'

But for us long-legged, far-sighted passengers, the cello has evolved into the ideal traveling companion, one who doesn't cough or go potty and one who saves us lots of bucks.

Boomerang

Affliction 1.

I had an operation on my wrist to repair a torn ligament and was undergoing painful wrist therapy. For at-home wrist rehab, my therapist supplied a huge wad of orange putty for me to massage.

Affliction 2.

My last name is Anderson. This affliction I share with some 900,000 U.S. residents and particularly, with one Gloria Anderson, who moved into the apartment just vacated by me. Never mind that our first names are different or that the appropriate address change info had been filed with the post office. The U.S.P.S. forwarded all her mail to me; her tax documents, checks, and bills. And when I repackaged her mail and resent it to her, you guessed it, the mail just boomeranged back.

As a result of the Anderson affliction, Gloria Anderson drove two hours to my new home to retrieve her mail.

"Oh my god," she exclaimed when she walked in the door and saw the orange wad on my table, "Did you do this?" And without waiting for my answer, called someone named John who was to come with camera immediately.

Gloria Anderson, as it turns out, is a renowned art critic.

"What do you call this sculpt?" the art critic insisted. Now my wrist was a mess, but my head was not, and I was immediately on to the life-changing potential of this chance encounter. So I modestly answered, "An Homage to Fingers."

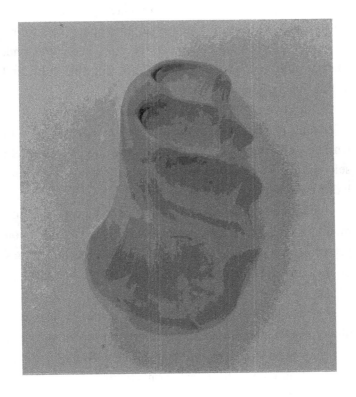

"Do you have more of these sculpts?" she asked hopefully.

"Of course," I replied, "And I shall assemble them here for you."

We made an appointment for a week hence for the unveiling of my art. (Oh how easily that adjustment from 'therapy' to 'art' was made.)

In the interim, my 'Homage to Fingers' appeared on the front page of the Covington Post.

A week is not a long time to create a life-time of art, but I was in high gear. I put in an emergency call to my hand therapist, asking her for all the putty she could find. She not only sent me the orange stuff, but blue stuff, and yellow, and green.

I discovered that 'An Homage to Fingers' was beginning to sag. Did I want to create ephemeral art *a la* Christo and Andy Goldsworthy? A big 'no.' I wanted to sell my art, so I needed to find a fixing spray which my hairdresser happily supplied.

I discovered that if you place what I now call 'my medium' on a non-plastic surface, it will stick. And if you pry if off, it will come with the all too plentiful collections of dust in my home. Thus, did I invent the marbleized effect.

I discovered that if you leave the medium outside at night, it will catch insects and perfectly preserve them.

And then I discovered that birds will feed on the insects, leaving beautiful beak-prints behind.

The life-long collection was growing larger by the hour. At first, I had difficulty in creating names. 'Cast off' because I created it first thing in the morning when I took my cast off. 'Splat' a work of art that fell from a shelf. Then I got with it. I named each piece and wrote the name large to help the art lover look smart. I ginned up blind and memorable emotion with names like *Jealousy, Anger,* and *Hate*.

Babies were oh so easy to suggest and so labeled. Neighbors on whom I tested my art would speak baby talk to these little baby-named sculpts.

The day before my second rendezvous with Gail Anderson, my mother announced her imminent arrival.

Now there are times when you really need a mother and there are times when you definitely don't. I knew my mom would blaze into my home, declare it a health hazard, and go after the orange stuff with a mop and garbage can.

I was catatonic with fear. She arrives. Ignores the bell and blazes in as predicted. But wait. She encounters a sculpt labeled *Baby Dan-Dan,* stops abruptly, and says in a super high voice, "Hewoe, wittie bittie, Dan, Dan. You are tho, tho thweet."

"Who made these?" she eventually asks. I am now catatonic with relief.

The next day, on schedule, Gloria Anderson arrives with crates, a team of packers to move my exhibit to the main hall of the Covington Museum, an armored car, and a tastefully designed little bag—to retrieve her latest batch of mail.

You're Never Too Old
to Learn

"Why are you so excited?" I asked Mom as she burst gleefully through the door. She had been shopping in Chicago while my husband and I were at work.

"I learned something important and I saved lots of money," she proclaimed.

"Okay, Mom, let's have it," I prompted.

"Well," she continued, "I got stopped by a policeman for driving through a red light and he asked me if I knew how to bribe a cop. I was embarrassed to answer *no*, but he kindly responded, 'No problem. I will teach you.'"

"Then he took my driver's license and a $20 bill from the wallet I had in my hand, wrapped the bill around my license, and told me to hand the combo to him. Then he returned my wallet and my license and said, before driving off, 'You're a very fast learner. Congrats!'"

The Not-Check-My Luggage Decision

Should I bring food on my United Airline flight? Or should I buy food on board? I decided to buy food on board because I was already wearing five sweaters and two jackets that I couldn't fit into my carry-on bags and had no way of carrying anything else. That is because I had not checked luggage, and that was because I didn't have time to arrive early to check it, and because I did not have an hour to spare retrieving it or perhaps, because I didn't want to pay the check-luggage fee.

So I decided, as I said, to buy food on board.

I contemplated the coach lunch menu. It was Inspirational. How bad can 'bean dip with Greek yoghurt and roasted pablano cheddar' be? You have no idea until you taste it.

How safe is eating stick cheese? The cheese expiration date is 2030. Its life span exceeds mine.

Do you crave protein? Well, go for 'Fiesta Chili Lime Dippers® with Olive Oil + Sea Salt Crackers—a culinary combination of luscious, tangy Fiesta, Chili Lime Dippers with whole grain goodness' for a 'grab-and-good® protein snack.'

Or How about Parmesan peppercorn spread?

The choice was agonizingly difficult.

This lunch was not free, you know. I had to pay for it. And with uncharacteristic forethought, I had stuffed cash in the pocket of my outermost jacket.

However, the flight attendant says cash doesn't work. "Cash doesn't work!" I blurted, "Did Uncle Sam hear you say that?" In truth, the last time I used cash was to pay a multi thousand bill for a new carpet; a mysterious condition of the bargain imposed by the carpet-store owner.

While I did have the forethought to store cash in my pocket in anticipation of paying for lunch, my credit card is in the luggage bin above and I am, of course, at the window seat. My fellow seatmates file out, so I can locate my credit card. Despite being almost immobilized by all my clothes, I find it, and get clumsily into my seat, spilling my drink.

As I feel the 'root-beer-float-with-marshmallow' penetrate through to my skin, I am forced to reconsider all my decisions *du jour*.

Wheat-Thin Addicts
V. Nabisco

Did you ever eat a Wheat Thin? The answer is 'No.' No one eats just one. I'm here to warn you that Wheat Thins are addictive and to also admit that I'm hooked. My addiction resulted from a sickness, which caused serious weight loss and which sidelined my exquisite and exorbitantly expensive wardrobe.

Post sickness, I embarked on a weight-gaining binge. Hello, Wheat Thins.

That's when I learned that those innocent-looking thin things are addictive.

After my weight was restored and my wardrobe was reactivated, I kept gorging on them. I pretended to go to the super market for yogurt and would come back with yogurt and eight boxes of you know what. I knew every grocery store that was open post-midnight. I started exercising five hours a day to negate my Wheat-Thin craze. Desperately, I started Wheat-Thin-Addicts Anonymous.

My house quickly filled up with other Wheat-Thin addicts. I tried to book space for our meetings in local churches like Alcoholics Anonymous and Sexaholics Anonymous do. But Wheat-Thin addicts got no respect, even though eight boxes of Wheat Thins contain 8,960 calories. I even got threatening emails from an angry observer who accused us of lampooning drug addicts and threatened to zap us to Mars.

After agonizing discussions, our group decided to pursue a practical solution to our Wheat-Thin addiction. We would stop Nabisco from making them. So we formed a delegation to visit Nabisco at its headquarters in New Jersey.

My fellow delegates included, both, a woman who attributed her toothlessness to the phytic acid contained in Wheat Thins and a man who, if he didn't have his Wheat-Thin fix, would go dangerously bonkers, shaking ordinary folks down on the street for their imagined Wheat Thins, which he was sure were concealed in their underpants.

We had no trouble gaining an audience with Nabisco's C.E.O. We presented ourselves as Wheat-Thin addicts, which he originally thought was a great thing but was overcome with guilt and remorse when he heard the genuine addiction that we said Wheat Thins caused.

He promised to have his scientists test for addicting ingredients.

He promised to poll the psychiatric community for Wheat-Thin addiction treatments. He promised to get back to us with his findings in no later than ten years.

Unsatisfied, we enlisted the aid of a lawyer among our always-growing addict group. He was convinced he could bring Nabisco to its knees in this, his first-ever case.

At his insistence, we posted a petition on the web and got, would you believe, ten million signatures, agreeing that Wheat Thins were addictive. Even Bugs Bunny signed on.

And then we subpoenaed Nabisco to 'recall and cease manufacturing the forenamed addictive product.'

We accused Nabisco of not only knowing that Wheat Thins were addictive, but of actively promoting the addiction. The accusation was supported by Nabisco itself, on its box, which invited shoppers to 'Taste the 100% irresistible 100% whole grain.'

Folks, 100% is not just a little irresistible. It is air tight irresistible. And aside from firing its box designer, there was little that Nabisco could do but comply with our cease and desist.

To you, fellow addicts, I say, grab Wheat Thins now, while they're still available, because they won't be for long. As for me, I have stocked all the Wheat-Thin boxes my house will hold and am planning to post them on e-bay for just $20 a box, while they last.

Crime Really Doesn't Pay

I have been mulling over a career change and this morning, from National Public Radio., I learned some career-changing news; only 5% of burglaries in the United States are ever solved. Holy Moly. Even risk-averse people like me can live with those odds. I only hope that this nation-wide revelation by N.P.R. will not cause a burglar market glut.

A 95% percent chance of not getting caught! Wow. And I bet the percentage is even higher for us college educated burglars.

So what to do? What to do? Make a business plan. Yes.

1. Find a fence.
2. Identify a victim.
3. Rob.
4. Unload goods to fence.
5. Collect cash.

But first, I must do more research. Much more. Better call work and take a flu leave. Okay. Here I go.

Googling 'fence.' All I find are steel and wooden things for commercial and residential properties.

Googling 'pawn shop.' Off to one near the bail office at the court house, just a few miles away. Learning the pawn process is easy. I just bring in my newly acquired valuables. They give me cash and they sell the goods. Easy, like I said.

Home again, with a great guitar I bought at the pawn shop at an unbelievably low price.

Now Googling 'burglary.' Find two promising entries: *Developing an F.B.I. Profile for Burglars* and A P.B.S. item on *How to Commit the Perfect Crime.* Will study these later. Yes.

Oh. Oh. Here is another N.P.R. story: *Burglaries on the Decline in the United States.* Why decline? How alarming and how counter-intuitive when the odds of success are so great.

Need to know.

Reading the story.

Learning the answer from Barry Mathis, a former burglar (former!) and practicing addict. Oh, Oh. Why Barry, why I wonder? He says he stopped breaking into homes because a burglar needs buyers, but everybody has everything now, and everybody only wants 'new.' He says, "There's just no money in it anymore."

Oh shit. I run to the phone and tell my boss that I've had a miracle cure, my flu is gone, and I'll be back at work tomorrow.

Cremation: Way to Go

"Let's get cremated," Bob said to me.

"Okay. When? I'm busy this afternoon."

Bob's cremation enthusiasm was inspired by a letter he received from the Trident Society promoting their *Free Pre-Paid Cremation*. What kind of crazy ass claim was that?

Not so crazy, as it turns out. Most cremators won't let you pre-pay. Their quoted rates are subject to change without notice. If your weight tops the 250-pound mark, you're charged more. If you die at home instead of at an institution, you're surcharged. If you die out of county, the price goes up. And how your ashes are delivered—in a fancy urn or paper box—will affect the cost.

With a pre-paid cremation, those prices are fixed. Go ahead and gain weight or move to Siberia, you are covered. Of course, if you pre-pay and the company you chose goes bankrupt, you or your heirs are screwed.

Well, deciding that our gullible children would be conned by so-called grief counselors into making expensive and stupid decisions, we took the pre-paid route. And thirty days after signing on, we received two large, ugly urns for our post-cremation remains.

The ugly urns include ugly plaques on which we have scribbled our names. But, problem: what to do with two large ugly urns in an apartment? Solution: they are now featured on our mantle and have become an unending source of unpleasant conversation.

We also received a packet of forms to fill out to guide our heirs. My favorite exercise was writing my own obituary and several variations thereof because of evolving events. For example, the phrase 'Mickie Winkler will be mourned by Gary Clack (first husband), Alex Winkler (second husband), and Daryl Gerber (third husband)' cannot be used if any of those grieving individuals predecease me. So, I had to create three versions in anticipation of their earlier demise.

The sentence 'When she unexpectedly expired, she was honorably serving on the city council of Menlo Lark' won't be accurate if, as expected, I am voted out of office at the first opportunity voters get.

The 'Born in N.Y.C. to undocumented immigrants who bribed their way into the American paradise' will not change. Nor will mention of all the academic honors and awards I invented.

I struggled with the inclusion of 'her defeat of an addiction to Wheat-Thins.' Would that help other Wheat-Thin addicts seek help?

I also struggled for an inspirational ending which currently reads,

'Mickie summed up her life in the words of Robert Louis Stevenson,

"Glad did I live and gladly die,
And I laid me down with a will."'

Inspirational? Yes, unless I get into a fatal accident or get assassinated before I get to lay me down. Nevertheless, it is comforting to know that my kids will be spared nitty-gritty decisions in the possible event of my death.

The Crazy Husband Club

Little did I think when I joined the Crazy Husband Club that I could compete for the annual Crazy-Husband-Contest-Prize. But there I was. A finalist on stage, being prompted by the moderator to "tell the audience just what exactly your husband does to qualify you for this coveted prize?"

"My husband," I said proudly, "carries heavy things that have wheels."

"Really? What else does he do?"
"He chews throat lozenges."

He yells at robocallers.

He puts masking tape on the crack in his eyeglass lens.

"On every occasion, at funerals and weddings," I added, now choking with embarrassment, "he wears white socks. A gasp of disbelief and admiration rose from the audience."

"Please tell us more about your extraordinary husband." The moderator was clearly envious.

I could feel the prize in the balance, so with muffled thanks to my husband, I recounted the winning event. "Yesterday," I said, "my husband had a wisdom tooth pulled and was instructed to ice his swollen cheek for 20 minutes at a time. Then, last night I rushed him to the emergency room, not because his extraction was a problem but because, believing *more is better,* he iced his cheek for an hour instead, and gave himself what the doctor solemnly diagnosed as 'self-induced frostbite.'"

The clap meter registered 100 and the coveted Crazy Husband Prize was mine.

How lucky am I to have an award-winning crazy husband?

Making My PC 'PC'

My reporting is rated *not* politically correct. I've been rejected by literary journals for being offensive and tasteless and for putting their journals at risk. And I've had to take these objectionable objections seriously if I wish to succeed.

My first response was to make my PC 'pc.'

My computer is now programmed to change 'Merry Christmas' to 'Merry Holidays' and 'Founding Fathers' to 'Founding Founders.'

'Queer' gets changed to 'gay.' How queer is that.

I now call females who deliver mail mailwomen.

An editor castigated me because I insensitively wrote 'died' instead of 'passed away,' and then castigated me again for writing 'Jesus passed away on the cross.' What to do?

The racial thing is really hard to deal with. A black person can call a white person 'whitey.' But a white person can't say 'blacky.' In fact, most blacks are brown and most whites, as the Indians correctly noted, are 'pale faces.' But this writer will henceforth adopt a colorless palette and go with Afro-American and Caucasian. And whoops, did I say 'Indians?' I mean Native Americans (who, by the way, migrated from Asia and are not native at all).

And to reaffirm my political correctness, let me be clear:

Whether you're smart or less smart,
whether you prefer dead vegetables to dead animals,
whether you want folks to carry concealed weapons or insist that weapons be visible,
Whether you think global warming (I mean climate change), is real or a hoax perpetrated by almost every scientist in the world

I just report what I see and, honestly, mean no offense.'

Misreading, Misleading
Travel Brochures

Would a week-long hiking, kayaking, and biking expedition in Alaska sound as exciting to you as it did to me? With Denali? And wild animals?

Well, let my self-delusional reading of the Alaska Adventure brochure inspire *you* to be a brochure-reading skeptic.

On the aforementioned Alaska all-sport 'Adventure,' for example, the brochure tells us that we head toward Denali, luxuriate in a Denali viewpoint and even stay one night at the Denali Perch Resort, but it failed to mention that we would never ever breach the Denali-Park boundary and actually get into Denali Park. And while 'eagles' may be 'a common sight in many parts of Alaska' as the brochure said, they were not frequent flyers on our route, nor did we spot any wild animals. One question addressed by the brochure was right-on,

Q: 'Will I be assaulted by a bear?'

Ans: 'No.'

Okay. So we sign up and assemble at seven a.m. at the Hampton Inn in Anchorage. If I had been the tour leader of this expedition, I would have wanted to prepare the group for the best possible experience, get group expectations in line with reality, and overcome the effects of the misleading brochure. So my kickoff would go something like this:

"Good morning, fellow travelers.

I am your hard-working and honest tour guide, not the advertiser who wrote the brochure that brings us here. So, listen up.

In this hotel, you can see stuffed bears, stuffed fish, and stuffed fox. If seeing wildlife is important to you, I suggest you look around, here, now. The observant among you may see some moose shit on the road. But scat is all the evidence of wildlife you'll see.

You have all come to see the spectacular scenery. Let me assure you, it is there and if you are extremely lucky and the clouds ever lift, you will actually see it. The weather? Well, it's Alaska. Do not be discouraged by the drizzle we are currently experiencing. Please, do not ask me when the rain will stop. At this time of year, the rain stops when the snow begins.

On this trip, you will see black-bird like creature buzzing around. In fact, they are not birds, they are mosquitoes. And they need to be talked about. They thrive on tourists. Like all of us natives, they welcome new blood to Alaska. Your clothes are no barrier. Deet to them is an aphrodisiac. The bruises you have no doubt noticed on the faces of people around here come from slapping themselves.

Welcoming new blood to Alaska

As for you all, you are a diverse group from all over the States. Some prefer biking and some prefer kayaking, but there is one thing you all have in common. Not one of you has asked for a reference on this trip.

Now let's get our adventure underway. Let's synchronize our bladders and let's hit the road. You have invested $3500 for the land part of this outing, which is a huge incentive to have a very good time."

But I was not the tour leader. No one gave the kickoff speech I, herein, proposed. After about four days into our all-sport expedition, our expectations and reality started to meld. We learned to like hiking, biking, and kayaking with mosquitoes in the rain. It did not snow. And we all have become better at reading brochures.

Outrageous Fortune

'The slings and arrows of outrageous fortune' converged on my folks last week when they sold their Silicon-Valley home for six times the purchase price! For making their outrageous fortune possible, they wish to acknowledge their benefactors.

My folks are grateful first and foremost to Facebook. not because of its word-spreading prowess, but because Facebook relocated one mile from their (ex)home and created more than 1500 hundred jobs in the process. The price of my folks home responded to this unexpected and fortunate event—by soaring.

They are grateful to the grim and grumpy group of anti-growth citizens in the city, to which, Facebook located for its opposition to increasing the housing stock; thus, assuring that the demand for housing far outstrips the supply.

Our government (that would be the Government of the United States) also gets much credit. That credit would be for lowering interest rates to zero (that's 0) and fomenting a housing bubble. Thanks, Fed.

More thanks to our federal government for its outrageously *discriminating* policy of making it ridiculous to rent if you can possibly afford to buy because there are so many tax incentives to home ownership.

I wish to add my own note of thanks to you the tax payers. As a result of their outrageous fortune, my folks can now afford to give me $28,000 tax-free dollars of their hard-won money every year.

Like a lot

Reliably Wrong

I'm a loser. I don't say this with bitterness. Nor do I hate myself. Being a loser is my life's role. I'm sort of a minor goddess of small misfortune, the kind who receives tickets for going fifteen mph in a ten-mph zone.

My friends always quiz me about my market activities. They solicit my advice, so they can avoid it. And they are right. My portfolio infallibly reflects stock-market peaks—by going down. I try pretending to be my own friend and avoid my own advice. But it just doesn't work. I can't cast a different shadow.

My first husband used to rely on me for directions. If I said, "Turn right," he would turn left. Then one day, 'right' was right. He furiously slammed his fist on dashboard and yelled, "Damn it. You're not reliable anymore." Lack of trust led to divorce number one.

My second husband decided to make book on my talents. He created a business called 'Reliably Wrong Inc.' Politicians, wanting to know which positions to support, were my most constant clients. For most people, success approaches the 50% mark. But my unreliability rating reached 90%. And that is all the inaccuracy I claimed.

90%
Reliably Wrong Rating
Certified by the Wrong Raters of America

Nevertheless, and as bad luck would have it, one nameless tycoon sued me over my bad advice, ruining my reputation and my usefulness to husband number two. Both the company and the marriage were dissolved.

Some people appreciate my charm. I was recently named by my community as Citizen of Year. My sponsor was the owner of the auto repair shop that I patronize. My dentist presented the award. And the proprietor from the Pest Control Service delivered a special speech. I met him after we found that the ant traps I placed all over the house were faulty. They contained the ant food that attracts the ants alright, but they lacked the poison that kills them.

My shrink taught me to not only be proud of my uniqueness, but to delight in it. After my second husband bolted, I ran the following dating-column ad,

'Let this lady be your personal lightening rod—
deflecting all danger from you.'

This ad turned out to be the top-response generator in the column's history. Happy hookers and femme fatales were all out-stripped by me.

My shrink also helped me understand that just one slip caused friends and spouses to lose faith in my bad luck. With self-knowledge comes change. I have designed a term-limit marriage contract, with a fixed expiration date. My marriages will no longer explode, they'll just lapse, while I conscientiously strive to improve my psyche and become 100% wrong.

The Downside of Power
A Failed Politician Speaks Out

"Hello, Madam Mayor," the policeman said to me with a smile. I got off my bicycle to return the greeting and he rhetorically asked, "Do you know what you just did? You crossed the railroad tracks after the gates were coming down."

"Usually," he went on, "I just give bikers a lecture, but I will make an exception for the mayor." He wrote me a ticket. Crossing the tracks was not my only transgression. I had voted against giving a precipitous salary increase to our town's police.

More costly than standing up to police, however, was standing up to the framers of our Heritage Tree Ordinance. I renamed this ordinance the 'Heritage Twig Ordinance' because it protects even the newest and tiny trees from nearby development. For this, I was accused of liking people more than trees.

There were the dog owners who wanted to use the Little-League Park for a dog park when it was not being used for baseball. When I warned that the park would become known as Poop Park, the dog owners disowned me.

And so it went. I was collecting opponents. I felt that if I ran for re-election, mine might be the only vote I'd get. Even my husband, who was sick of washing off the graffiti detractors sprayed on our house, promised to vote for someone, anyone, else. So, two-thirds through my term, I announced that I would not run again.

Now my detractors got worried. How do you control a politician that doesn't want to be reelected? You don't. I got a huge revenue-generating hotel approved, despite claims by vocal bird-lovers that an eagle may someday want to nest at the site.

With my cohorts, I hired a private contractor to run the city's swim program against the apoplectic opposition of the union. Today, ours is the best swim program in the county.

We built a restroom in the city's largest park, despite neighborhood fears that the homeless would overrun it. In fact, the only building that now bears my name is that restroom a name sanctioned by opponents because as one gloated, "When folks go to the toilet, they will think of you."

I was productive and getting stuff done. So, did I really not want to run? My (very) few fans pointed out that I was a shoo-in, that no matter how much politicians are vilified, they get re-elected 90% of the time.

But I was, nevertheless, determined to retire, before I got any more tickets and before my tires were slashed, again.

Why, God?

Look, I get the Garden of Eden story. God makes Adam. Adam wants a mate. God takes one of Adam's ribs and makes Eve. Then God tells Adam and Eve to eat anything *except* fruit from the Tree of Knowledge. A serpent convinces Eve to eat from it. She does. Then he does. And the human race goes downhill from there.

But here's what I don't get. I don't get why God punished Eve for her transgression by saying, "I will surely multiply your pain in childbearing."

Now women don't write much about childbirth, but believe me, it is one big ouch.

And it seems to me that when God fashioned humans and made the female birth canal tiny, while making the fetus head huge, he did enough pain making. And then to intensify the pain because Adam and Eve ate a fruit just doesn't seem fair.

How AT&T and Comcast
Made My Doctor Rich
Part 1: Disconnecting from AT&T

Last November 28th, I celebrated my severance from AT&T; not as an employee, but as a customer. Yes!

The severance was prescribed by my doctor. He said I had stress-tested positive for AT&T. He said that years of dealing with its fantasy-billing and customer-disservice departments had put me at risk for chronic indigestion and even stroke.

Following his prescription, I eagerly returned the AT&T equipment, paid what I owed, and then gave a big party to commemorate and finalize the parting of ways.

But the Ghost Department of AT&T continued to haunt me.

The monthly billings persisted and grew to $2000. Late charges mounted. They even increased the cost of cable T.V., which I, of course, no longer received.

Indigestion returned.

My doctor pronounced AT&T an affliction with no known cure. He tried to have it labeled by the F.D.A. as a public health risk, along with dengue fever and syphilis.

Finally and by an ingenious method that I'm writing a book about, I did get hold of someone at AT&T who spent two hours on the phone with me reversing all the bogus charges.

The Kicker

But there is yet another chapter to the sickening part of the AT&T tale.

AT&T asked me to take a phone survey at the end of my two-hour phone ordeal. I wanted to take that survey so the young man who worked to have the charges reversed would get the heroic recognition he deserved.

The survey said, 'On a 1 is the worst, use your dial pad to rate the performance of your customer service representative.'

'Dear reader, take a look at the dial pad on your phone, and please, find me a 10!

The best I could rate my young hero was a 9.

And my doctor declared that mental health be added to the list of AT&T hazards.

Part 2: The Comcast Affliction

After disconnecting from AT&T, I signed on to the only other internet/cable option available at my home. Comcast. And I now understand why AT&T is only rated number two in the list of worst U.S. companies.

I had trouble with Comcast from the moment the technician arrived for my free installation and charged me for the cable required to connect the outside cable box to my T.V.

"Can I use my own modem?" I asked him.

"Yes, of course, you can supply your own modem," he said, "But [and he winked] if you don't rent ours, do not call with your many Comcast problems, because we can't help."

The first among those many problems occurred two days after Comcast was installed, when friends (now ex-friends) came to my Super Bowl Party. We got to see four hours of a struggling screen, frequently interrupted by the message, 'Oops. We are trying hard to restore your service.'

When I was diagnosed with Chronic Comcast-induced Indigestion, my doctor took a new tack. He designed the 'ComcATT Weight-Loss Program,' in which, he demonstrated that customers of Comcast and AT&T lose their craving for food and ability to retain it. He prescribed Comcast and AT&T for weight loss.

And the Winners Are?

As for AT&T and Comcast, are they repentant for the indigestion and weight loss they are now known to cause? No. They now advertise that customers who sign up on doctor's orders can deduct their bills from their taxes, as a medical expense, and their signups have surged.

Car Convert

I bought me a sports-car convertible armed with a floor shift, yeah. And felt the need to be aggressive, despite the road congestion where I live. I got to show off my car's prowess by deftly weaving in and out of lanes. Ginned up, big-time road rage. Yeah. But the rage was mine when those guys cut off sailed past me—always finger up—'cause I failed to predict correctly which lane would prevail.

The horn became my most aggressive tool. Drivers who didn't gas it when the light changed, would be emphatically honked. Distracted, phone-speaking drivers got conversation-ending blasts. With my horn, I could make jay walkers run. Yeah. Even old ones.

Then I was stopped for illegal horn blowing. My invocation of the 'reasonably necessary' exception to the horn- blowing rule, didn't work. Damn! Screw the horn. I installed Xenon headlights. And when I flashed my Xenons, I could make drivers pull right off the road. Cool. Until one pulled into a lamp-post.

Have you noticed how long traffic lights take to change? Infuriating! I bought me a light *Preempter,* an illegal device that can change red lights to green. And I mounted it in the grille of my car. Yeah. Cops didn't notice but burglars did. The damn thing was stolen. And my insurance agent laughed when I filed a claim.

I used to wear a sports cap when driving. Then I got sick of seeing my sagging, grim face on tickets from those traffic-enforcement cams. So I ditched the cap for a ski mask. And I also got sick of taking those on-line driving courses, you know, the courses you take to have points from your record removed? It takes eight hours to go through each damn course. No shit! When I did the math, I discovered that's like stopping for circa 480 lights. Hmmm. That did it.

I traded my sports car for a goody-two-shoes Prius, learned to steer the thing with my knees, moved my office onto the passenger seat, and am no longer distracted by traffic lights.

An Ultimatum to My Hip

Hey, Hip.
Stop giving me pain.
Stop making me look old.
Stop stopping me from playing pickle ball.
Stop! Or...I'll—I'll—what?
I'll replace you!

COP: Controlling Over-Population

Folks. Face up! Overpopulation is like the scourge of the planet. Old Malthus warned us: Overpopulation creates scarcity, famine, disease, war, and global warming. And who is talking about it? If you said *no one*, you'd be right.

I come to you tonight as president of COP, an organization committed to *Controlling Over-Population*.

And I'm here to tell you that this is a no-fooling-around issue. To reverse it, we need to take control. Henceforth, we propose to limit people—all people—men, women, priests, etc., to two kids each. Once you reach your kid quota, you get sterilized. Get it. No more kids. It's over. And if you lose one, you get a replacement at a foster home.

No more giving birth to unwanted children. We make morning-after pills free. In order to reach absolutely everyone, we force drug dealers to also distribute *the pill* with whatever else they sell.

And we expand abortion clinics. We give anti-abortionists the right to choose; between silence or changing their minds.

And how do we enforce population control policy? In the United States, that's simple. The National Security Agency (N.S.A.) has eyes and ears on phones, our emails, and on our computers. Make a call to a gynecologist? Buy a pregnancy test kit? Complain about morning sickness? Like Santa Clause, the N.S.A. will know and note.

As for outside the U.S.A., like in nations where many don't have tracking devices, COP wants to make them rich, get them cell phones, and then get the N.S.A. on their case. And just so you know, members of COP are adamantly opposed to the invasion of privacy by the N.S.A. except when it comes to sex and the conception of kids.

The Hail Mary

My Russian student brought me an article from the paper and asked, "Teacher, vut does zees mean?"

The article was headlined 'Hail Mary Fails.'

"Is szat like 'hello Mary?'" he asked.

I tried to explain the football article and, please excuse me, fumbled my first attempt, "No, you see, Mary is the Virgin Mary," I explained.

He looked confused. I went on: "The Virgin Mary is the mother of Jesus," His irritation was turning to anger.

"Virgin? Mother? You be makeeng fun of me?" he asked. I was making matters worse, so I took another tack.

"'Hail Mary' is the beginning of a prayer," I said.

He took the ball and continued incredulously, "To Mary, virgin, mother of Jeesus?"

"Look. This article means that the team was losing, time was running out, and in one desperate effort to win the game, the quarterback prayed to the Virgin Mary and then threw a long pass into the end zone, hoping to win the game."

My student, who actually liked American football, now understood the meaning of the phrase. But he pushed his luck.

"How can mother be virgin?" he asked.

"Okay," I said, "She was impregnated, not by her husband, but by the Holy Ghost."

My student got excited. "Really? Szat ees vunderfull! But," he added thoughtfully, "I hope my girl-friend don't *pull szat* on me."

Honest Dad, it was the Holy Ghost

Adulting

'Adulting' is a real new word.

'Adulting' is a good thing.

It means 'acting like an adult.'

It is not to be confused with adultering.

My intro to *'adulting'* came when my 26-year old asked me for Adulting-School tuition.

"Just $19.95 a month for an online course," he said.

"And what will you learn at Adulting School?"

"Adulting School," he recited from his brochure, "Teaches you how to cook and clean house, manage your finances, change a tire, fold a fitted sheet, and other important tools of self-reliance."

"You don't need to fold a fitted sheet," I protested, "Just put it back on the bed after washing it."

"Well," he argued, "Sometimes, I wash it one day and dry it several days later, so I use my second fitted sheet and have to fold the first."

I was beginning to see the Adulting- School need.

"And what financial skills will you learn?"

"Well, like how to balance a checkbook," he said.

"Did you miss that part of first grade where you learn to add and subtract?"

"Well, not exactly how to manage a checkbook but how not to spend more than I earn and how to take out a loan if I do spend more than I earn, so I don't build up exorbitant finance charges on my credit card."

"You need to learn that, do you?"

"And what part of cleaning house don't you understand? From what I surmise about your apartment is that you worship mess and dirt."

"I know my place is a mess from the way friends cringe when they come by, so I need to clean it."

"Why not allot the time to cleaning your home that you allot to Adulting School? Your home would be immaculate," I wisely offered.

He offered a counter idea, "Why not save the money you would spend on my Adulting-School tuition and let me move in with you?"

Now, I love my son full-time, but I love him most when he's somewhere else. After a super-long pause in which I exhibited zero enthusiasm, he added, "And I'll pay you what I now pay in rent, so we can hire a cleaning service." Bingo. Jackpot. Sold! In truth, I share my son's abhorrence for house cleaning. I just don't share his tolerance for dirt.

"Will you promise to work on adulting skills if I say okay?" I asked.

"Yes, yes, mommy, I promise," he said, and he crossed his heart and swore.

How to Remove a Rattle in Your Car

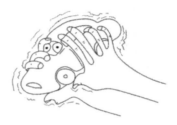

My Audi TT developed a rattle. It emanated from the tonneau cover, you know, the cover on sports cars that hides the mess in your trunk from view.

The rattle was driving me crazy. "Crazier," my husband interjects.

It was so annoying and noisy that my son threatened to no longer borrow my car.

I learned on the internet that I was not alone in suffering from tonneau-cover mania. I also learned that the tonneau cover for my car is neither fixable nor replaceable, even from junk yards.

What to do?

- Remove the tonneau cover and expose the mess? Not acceptable.
- Learn to live with the rattle? Not possible.

But a third and successful option emerged. A hypnotist suspended my ability to hear the rattle and other noises emanating from the trunk.

The upsides are that for me:
- There is no rattle,
- But for my son, the rattle still exists.

The downside is that should rattle snakes take up residence in my trunk, I may fail to notice them.

The Making of 27 U.S. Citizens

And One English Teacher

There we were. Twenty-eight non-English -speaking students eager to learn English and one novice, monolingual teacher. That would be me.

My post-retirement plan was to teach conversational English abroad. To launch this plan, I was told I needed experience. To get experience, I contacted the local Travelers Aid. My two qualifications were that

1) I could speak English and

2) I could take the 2 p.m. class that very day.

My Class was comprised mostly of Vietnamese, but included immigrants from all parts of the globe.

The youngest Vietnamese was a 15-year-old who was not allowed to dance at home and would not stop dancing in class.

The oldest Vietnamese introduced himself as Trang Gonzalez.

"Gonzalez!" I insensitively blurted, "What kind of a Vietnamese name is that?" And he told me, "Leave Vietnam. Come to Los Angeles. I happy, happy, happy to come. Choose most common name in Los Angeles phone book; Gonzalez."

There was a Russian oboist who would complain, "Meekey, I am learning to speeek English vit Vietnam accent."

There was the lone Italian who waved his arms Italian style when speaking Italian and turned into a stone when trying English speech. Every day, this Italian was fifteen minutes late to class until one memorable day, when he entered and athletically proclaimed, "*Io sono presto*! (I am early!). *Io sono solo dieci minuti ritardo*! (I am only ten minutes late!)."

A military general told us he was from Rangoon in Burma, immediately prompting another general to say he was from Yangon in Myanmar. Check your map to find out that these are, in fact, the very same place, forcing me to keep these generals far apart.

With lots of *je ne sais quoi*, I finally understood that, above all else, the members of my class (except for the dancing teenager) were focused on becoming U.S. citizens. I am proud to say that by the time my students left the class, all but the dancer had the bizarre tools necessary to pass the citizenship test, even if they still could not make a phone call or interview for a job.

In my class, they learned to recognize and use such important words as *habitually* and a*dvocated*. They learned that *right* was something *inalienable*, and did not mean *correct* or *a turn*. They could answer profound questions like:

How many voting members does the House of Representatives have?[1] or How many amendments are in the U.S. Constitution?[2] They could spell *Massachusetts*. They already knew *that the last day you can send in federal income tax forms is April 15th*. In short, they were exquisitely prepared to execute the privileges and duties of citizenship and I was similarly prepared to teach conversational English abroad[12].

*** 36%

---

[1] 27
[2] 435

America: The Awesome Land of Laws

America is a land of laws and our state legislators do an awesome job by passing some 40,000 new laws each year. Remembering that *ignorance of the law is no excuse*, I try to keep track of them all.

While I try to keep track of all the laws, I, sometimes, fail and get arrested or fined—like the time I ran afoul of Skamania County law in Wisconsin and did a legal no-no by harassing Big Foot.

Luckily, in Portland, Oregon, I tied my illegally untied shoelace just as a cop was coming to ticket me. And speaking of lucky, in Indian Wells, California, I was caught red-handed drinking cement. I was about to be arrested, when the cop got a call on his radio, and before speeding off in his squad car, proclaimed, "Today is your lucky day. Someone has just been murdered." I felt lucky indeed!

California, where I live, passes the most laws of any state. We are awesome Number1. And we should be, because our legislators are the most highly paid. Why, in California, alone, we pass some 1,000 laws each year! Wow.

How come? Well, our legislators are rated by the number of laws they sponsor, which is good because it shows they are working hard for us. So, they pass important bills to improve society, like the bill mandating that seat belts be worn in charter buses (not to be confused with the law that says you have to wear seat belts in all buses, period).

We, savvy Californians, have spawned a whole new industry, designing low-impact laws that won't piss anyone off. Need a needless law? Comb through ours.

To get a law passed, our legislators join an 'I'll-vote-for-your-law-if-you-vote-for-mine' buddy system. This is important because laws typically run about 30 pages each, and if all the legislators read all the laws, they would have to read about 30,000 pages each year, like the complete set of the Encyclopedia Britannica. What a waste of time. Only the governor who signs the laws must read them all.

Sometimes, almost no one gets to read a law because of an emergency process called 'Gut and Amend.' Say some especially urgent matter comes up at the end of a legislative session and there is no time for proper vetting. Then one impending law that is cleared for passage is gutted and another, more important law, is plopped in its place. Like when the law governing information on tuberculosis-testing results was urgently replaced by the bill requiring cities to hire union labor. I was a little concerned about this because tuberculosis is a big-time bad and very infectious disease. But I think that the new bill must be okay because the legislators passed it and the governor signed on.

Living in San Francisco, as I do, is especially awesome. Last year, I got to vote on 17 state ballot measures, 23 San Francisco city ballot measures, and 1 regional ballot measure. Wow. That's 41 ballot measures, plus 13 candidates for a very grand total of 54 votes. I helped decide things like whether men had to wear visible condoms during the filming of pornographic films. Bet you wonder how that vote turned out.

Happily, there is no time-limit in the voting booth. And note that while food deliveries to the booth are verboten, you can bring all the food and drinks you need while exercising your voting privilege.

Friends, I just hope my awe and enthusiasm for our law-making process has rubbed off on you. And rest assured. Most laws exist forever because they are almost impossible to remove, once passed.

German Dogs Don't Like Us

We once had a German shorthair pointer named Manfred. Don't let the past tense fool you. Manfred is no doubt still alive, just alive somewhere else. He was last seen with a dead cat in his mouth, which he had been carrying around, proudly for days. Was it a bobcat? No. A feral cat? No. Alas, it was the neighbor's pussy cat.

After that, we had a German shepherd named Aldrik. Aldrik also left. In fact, we had taken Aldrik to an obedience trainer who lived four hours away. We agreed to pay $400 upfront and $400 post training for a three-month session at obedience boarding school. Graduation time arrives. Aldrik, my husband, and I are reunited at the trainer's school. To demonstrate Aldrik's new obedience skills, the trainer proudly released him into the woods. He waited five minutes and then whistled for him to obediently return. Nothing. Ten minutes. Nothing. Feeding time. Nothing. It was the last we saw of Aldrik.

"So what is our takeaway from these runaway experiences?" my husband and I asked ourselves.

"We saved $400," he offered.

"German dogs don't like us," I countered, "Ergo, we should not have German dogs."

"Or," my husband added, "We should not have any dogs with legs."

Getting Old Is Getting to Be a Full-Time Job

Getting old has become a 24/7 job. I spend much time tracking my contraptions, like glasses, so I can find my dentures, which I realize, are missing when it hurts to eat crunchy cereal.

If I see people moving their lips, I'm reminded that I forgot to wear my hearing aids. The beeping of hearing aids reminds me that I forgot to change the hearing-aid batteries. And when the shower sounds especially loud, I am reminded that I forgot to take out my hearing aids before getting into the shower and that they are about to be destroyed. A good day is when I remember that I forgot to lock the car.

My dermatologist warns me to wear sunscreen before going near a window. To which, the eye doctor coolly includes 'shades.' To compensate for the lack of direct sun, my internist adds vitamin D to my daily pile of medications. I think all these pills explain why I'm gaining weight.

The number of phone calls I receive is expanding, even as my pool of friends shrinks. I get calls from Nigerians in jail who need money; from I.R.S. agents threatening to sue whomever answers the phone; from fire-fighters and police chiefs who politely ask for my credit card number, without even trying to justify the ask.

Do I feel sorry for myself as my getting-old chores increase? You bet, until I remember the plus side; when checking through airport security, I no longer need to take off my shoes.

No wonder I'm gaining weight

The Dawning of the Light

Can you believe? My kid's ambition is to work for the United States Post Office.

"Why, Barry?" I quiz him, "The U.S.P.S. is a dying institution or should be, I say. It is losing us taxpayers billions of dollars."

"Well," he recites, as 10-year-olds can do, "Because I would get higher pay than in the private sector, I would have the very best health care, I would receive an unexcelled sprension (he meant 'pension'), and I could never be fired, even if I ate ice-cream on the job."

"But" I argue, "The U.S.P.S. may be privatized like in New Zealand and Sweden and other places, where service improved and the work force was cut by one-third."

"That will never happen here!" my 10-year-old kid tells me.

"How do you know that?" I persist,

"Because a union guy came and spoke to us at school."

"Mom, the union guy said he once met you. He said you met at your congresswoman's office, that you were complaining that all the mail for the neighborhood was dumped in your mail box and you had to deliver it to the neighbors yourself."

"That is true. I remember. But how could *he* remember *me*? After the congresswoman transmitted my complaint, he told her to stuff it and just walked out."

"He said he remembered. He said to tell you "Sorry." Sorry that when you ran for City Council, your campaign mailers weren't delivered until 2 days after the election."

"That's true, too. None of my mailers were delivered, and I lost the election. Hmmm, but, Barry, what about your ambition to be an astrophysicist?"

"Well, I'd rather be a postman because I can make as much money and I don't even have to go college. The union guy said he would come by the house and talk more about it to me."

"You didn't tell him where we live or that we moved?" I asked, hopefully, "I didn't have to. He said he knows where I live now."

The Winners Will Win

Ladies and gentlemen, politicians and aspiring politicians, let me welcome you to the first annual *Getting to the Winners Circle* seminar, sponsored, of course, by our new political party, The Winners.

Who are The Winners? We are mature seniors, who put love of country first and have happily been paying sales taxes, income taxes, property taxes, capital gains taxes, double-jeopardy dividend taxes, and social security taxes dam near forever.

Why are you so concerned about what we Winners want? Why have you each paid $1000 to attend this seminar? It's because you know that seniors are the most cohesive voting bloc in this country. You know that your future in politics depends on us—that what we Winners want, we Winners will get. We've taken out our bayonets, turned up our hearing aids, and we're ready to restore sanity to this land.

First, we shall clear up a common misconception, espoused by an eminent politician who will soon be returned to private life. He said, "Seniors do not want to burden the next generation with a deficit."

To this eminent politician, we say, "Why the hell not?"

Enough. Let us give you vote-hungry people an idea of what we seniors *will* support and invite you to look at the world through new (aging) eyes.

Frankly, we are ashamed to admit that those self-serving, squabbling politicians now in-charge of our country are our kids. We would spank them if spanking were still allowed. But we still can teach them a lesson as embodied in the first goal of our program, which is to **enact the Really-Real-Truth-In-Politics Act.** How radical is that? And we've got a tech-savvy way to achieve it.

You know how some of us who have had heart surgery wear pacemakers? And some of us who were released early from jail wear ankle monitors? Well, we will require all candidates and elected officials to wear small, embedded lie detectors. We selected lie detectors that are configured to emit loud delightful sounds of laughter whenever a lie is told. We are convinced that with this Act, existing politicians and aspiring politicians, such as those of you who still remain in our audience, will actually give a hoot about their constituents and about the future of America. And predict that political debates will achieve reality-show T.V. ratings when the lie-detecting requirement kicks in.

Second, we propose to eliminate all U.S. participation in war, cold turkey. Please, please. Hold your applause. Instead of trying (and failing) to liberate places like Afghanistan and Iraq, we'll liberate the billions (and billions and billions) of dollars we spend.

Eliminating our participation in war is a platform item we all can love. Parents who have children will love this. As will people who say they support Right to Life. Environmentalists understand that the best way to stop inflicting damage on the environment is to stop dropping those damn carbon-emitting bombs. And we, seniors, would love to replace the Department of Defense with the Department of Senescence.

Third, we propose to increase the voting age to 35. By so doing, we eliminate the vote of those with no taxable income and are, thus, perfectly willing to tax everyone else. Also, having eliminated war, we eliminate the stupid argument that 'if they're old enough to fight, they're old enough to vote.'

Folks, we are sure that when you look deeply into your hearts and wallets and at the polls, you will find ways to love and run on this platform. We are sure you will join us in saying that *Everyone Will Be Winners When the Winners Win.* We are sure that any rival's call to 'defeat The Winners' will fail.

And we look forward to welcoming you to the Winners Circle, come Election Day.

How can you defeat
«The Winners»
???

Outing Sid Jacobs

Before I out Sid Jacobs, I will tell you who he is. He is an amazingly well-known denizen of New York City. If you go to a restaurant, any restaurant, and tell the *maître d'* that Sid Jacobs sent you, you will be escorted past the waiting line of customers and seated immediately.

If you want to rent a New York apartment, the name Sid Jacobs will get you both first consideration and then bottom price. If you want to get the attention of publishers, as did I, for this very piece, you will tell them Sid Jacobs insisted I contact you. *Voici*! And note, should you ever invoke the name of this famous man, be sure to convey his sincere regards. So where did I meet Sid Jacobs? In bed. That's the unabashed truth. About twenty years ago, I was desperate to take my clients to the Russian Tea Room for dinner, per the client request. I had called the Tea Room to reserve a table and learned it was over-reserved. So, lying there, in bed, I concocted Sid Jacobs. And since then, he has been my un-aging and constantly reliable friend.

Famous photo of Sid Phillips taking a shower

Matchless.com

I was recovering at home from an illness, kind of loopy from meds, lonely, and bored. So, I decided to sign up for Match.com.

For starters, Match.com instructs me to present a personality portrait, so I composed this beautifully deceitful description of my calm and loving self, denied having children (mine are Medicare ready), grabbed an online photo from Stock Photos, knocking forty years off my age.

Then I got to Match.com's *Check Out and Pay* page with an automatic renewal clause. Well, I had faked everything about me, all, of which, was acceptable to Match.com, but my fake credit card didn't pass. So I gave up on Match.com. But Match didn't give up on me.

It sent me sent tempting, sample solicitations from guys (?) in the age group (?) of 'my' interest.

There was the Frenchman, George. From his self-adoring-self depiction, it is obvious he doesn't need a mate because he has himself.

Hank (5102) is 58. Doesn't have kids but 'definitely wants them.'

Or how about 'tall, dark, and handsome' Benzilla (529), who writes,

'I have too many special projects going on to go out and meet someone new.' I wonder if Benzilla529, who is too busy to go out, realizes that he is paying Match.com circa 25, automatically renewing dollars each month.

My attempt to 'unsubscribe' went un-honored. Unsolicited emails announcing that men 'were winking at me' clogged my inbox. My smart phone sounded like a pop-corn making machine. Spam would not accept Match.com emails. Replying to the never-ending messages always brought me back to *the Check out and Pay* page.

How to terminate the Match.com affair? Aha. I couldn't turn Match.com off, but, yes, I could change my profile. I now present as a '90-year-old woman seeking a kidney match.' And I am, once again, lonely and bored.

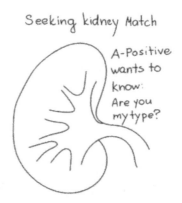

The New Robot Test

Once upon a time, when robots were just being born, a man named Alan Turing devised a test. He would have a real live human being and a robot, both off-stage, each answer the same question. The audience had to decide who (or should I say which) they thought the human speaker was.

Well, folks, those days are over. We speak to robots all the time. Sometimes, we know we are speaking to robots and sometimes, we do not. My husband yells at them on the phone.

Robots like Siri give you 'how to get here and there' navigation directions and are exasperated when you miss a turn. I swear, Siri once called me a dummy, though my husband insists it was my own (but, oh, so accurate) inner voice.

The other day, I bumped into a robot delivering food on my sidewalk. It said, "Excuse me," when I inadvertently blocked its path and then said, "Thank you," when I moved. Did I then say, "No problem?" Yes, I did.

I have just used the word 'it' referring to a robot but, well, *it* sounds so mechanical. 'It' just doesn't feel right. So what should we call our quasi-human machines? 'Robos?' And what if you get confused and call a human a robo? What if you called me a robo? Would I get mad? Or would I take it as a compliment?

There are male and female-looking robots. My bonafide male friend thinks that a male robot should be called 'Robot' and the female should be called 'Robette.' But I think 'Robo' should apply to both, given our push to obliterate the male-female difference.

So, back to Turing's question. How should we test to see whether the thing or person with whom/which we are dealing is human? And the answer is: Does it giggle when you tickle it?

Which one is real?

A Body Camera for Billy?

"Mom, I want a body camera for my birthday."

"A body camera?"

"Yes, like the police wear, so I can take videos of what's happening."

"But, Billy, those body cameras don't work. They fail all the time."

"Why do you say that, Mom? Uncle Joe showed me that the company making them says they are infallible."

"Well, you ask Uncle Joe about the case in Utah in which a driver at a traffic stop was injured by three police officers and all three cameras worn by the police officers failed. Even the dash cams on both their squad cars failed as well. Or ask Uncle Joe about the case in Albuquerque, where all five police cameras malfunctioned at the same time. You know, Billy, those cameras are expensive!"

"But, Mom, we have full footage of the case here in Palo Alto. We can see the police breaking down the door of a guy for driving with a suspended license, dragging him from the house, and beating his head on the hood of his car. That camera worked."

"Billy, that video was taken by the victims own security camera, not a body or dashboard cam. In fact, the squad cars *did* have dashboard cams but all three were parked out of camera sight."

"Uncle Joe said I could make money by selling my videos to T.V. stations."

"Billy, that's dangerous. You ask Uncle Joe about Ramsey Orta. He took pictures of a cop choking Eric Garner to death for selling cigarettes on the street without a license. Orta went to jail soon after on various charges. Even *his mother* was threatened with arrest, so I don't want you doing that."

"Mom, instead of a body cam, could I get a photography drone."

The French and
Their Language

I don't mind *French*—the language.

I just mind *The* French—who worship their language.

They get upset with people who mangle it.

They even get upset when you imitate a French accent and the imitation is bad.

Of course not all French people are language intolerant. Some are kind and helpful and will even answer your questions in English, which most of the French have learned. But the bad things in life are what we most remember, like operations and traffic tickets and being humiliated in France.

My first foray into France was on a bicycle. I was biking from Genoa, Italy to Nice (in English, niece). It was pouring. Almost immediately after entering France, I found a shelter, which I shared briefly with a very wet Frenchman. He asked, "*Parlez-vous française?*"

To which, I humbly answered in French, "*Un peu,*"—"a little."

His response, "*Un **petit** peu.*" And you know what '*petit*' means, *n'est pas*? I spoke two little words in response to his question and he zinged me with an insult. Whereupon, preferring the rain to me, he left.

Folks, I speak a lot of languages badly, not just French. When I need help, the Russians laugh at my bad grammar and then help me. The Chinese correct my tones and then help me. But the French? The French get angry. I once asked directions of a Frenchman in Paris. Do you know what he yelled? He yelled, "*Arrêtez!*" That means *stop*. In other countries, you get brownie points for trying. In France, you get put down.

Don't get me wrong. Having taught English to foreigners, I know it is a crazy-hard language to learn. There is whole book in Russian on when to use English articles like 'and,' 'the,' 'an,' or 'a.' My admonition to my students? "It's okay to make mistakes as long as you can express the thought." But for the French, it's not what you want to say. It's the way that you say it.

French was once the *lingua franca*. Now, English is the *lingua franca*. Russian was damn near the *lingua franca* and Chinese may be next. I am convinced that the English language became the lingua franca not only because the English colonized so many parts of the world and because the United States emerged as the superpower after the world wars, but also because Americans are unrepentantly monolingual.

The United States has not elected a president fluent in a language other than English in 87 years. And we recently elected a president with an English vocabulary so limited and repetitious that even my foreign students could easily understand what he said.

I think maybe the French are kind of pissed, not just because we Americans don't know French or because we decimate their language, but because our language has eclipsed theirs.

So what to do when I next visit Paris? Should I rent a dog and be like everyone else? Should I double kiss everyone I meet on the cheek, Parisian style? Should I stop wearing my T-Shirt that says 'California wines are Number 1'?

Or should I just chill out, enjoy the sights and the food, and If I need a bathroom or if I've lost my hotel, instead of sticking my chin out, I'll take my friendly phone out, and ask Google (or Siri) for help.

Me3

Fellow Females,

Are you fed up with being the only sex to bear children?

And the only sex being told when you can abort?

Are you sick of, well, being under men?

Are you angry about the centuries spent being non-persons, deprived of the right to own property, to sign contracts, to control your own meager wages, and of course, deprived of the right to vote?

Black men got their voting rights in 1870. We black and white women got ours in 1920.

Do you think we deserve reparations for all these man-made inequities?

Well, I certainly do, but thinking won't recompense us for centuries of abuse. Power will. Let's take it. Do you know that voting women now outnumber voting men?

By using our hard-earned voting rights, we could empty all men from all chambers of power. We could move on to Me3.

Not only would we award ourselves reparations, we would make America great again. Imagine a nation without testosterone-driven politics; a world of free trade, in which everyone benefits, one free of self-censored speech, a nation, in fact, of free love. We could replace the Department of Defense with the Department of Peace and stop sending our kids off to fight needless, never-ending wars. We could pass a law doubling the number of lady's rooms is public places. Yes. In our nation, the goddess replaces the god. Why not?

While we prepare for this political transformation, it will take at least ten years to totally empty the senate of men, we can pursue power-taking strategy number two. Remember Lysistrata? She was the Greek heroine who organized women in the warring city-states of Sparta and Athens to, now get this, withhold sex until a negotiated peace between the city states was achieved. And she did it before there was social media.

We can employ the Lysistrata method for immediately achieving those reparations. We offer 'Bang for Power.' It's as simple as that.

Men who oppose my idea sanctimoniously say, "You will soon become as corrupt, despicable, and power-hungry as men are."

To which, I say, "We shall very soon see."

Everybody Wins

I am so excited. I just received a phone call from the Police Officers Union asking for a donation. A few minutes before, I had received a call from the Police Benevolent Union, also asking for cash. Were either of these organizations real? Yes, they were. With some expert sleuthing, I learned that both were part of the International Union of Police Associations, AFL-CIO, which qualified as one of the fifty worst charities in the U.S. of A.—a charity, basically, that distributes very little of what it takes in.

How incredibly inspirational! I have been searching a long time for a super-profitable career, and after studying the fifty worst charities, and seeing the millions some C.E.Os make, have determined that I could apply my brilliant analytical skills to the charity-creation job.

The fifty worst charities list taught me so much. It taught me that worst charities, above all, need a good name, a convincing name, one that sounds familiar. It taught me that most of the fifty worst were gut-wrenchingly named for distressed children, followed by charities with 'police' or 'fire' in the name.

And, of course, a fair number referenced religion.

I decided not to pursue the distressed children angle. I am too moral and too sensitive- and the competition is too great.

But police were fair game. How about targeting rich single-family neighborhoods with the name *Your Neighborhood Police Fund*? Sounds friendly and sincere. Right? The slogan could be 'You remember us and we'll remember you.' As a driver who sometimes confuses yellow lights with green lights, I would surely give to that.

And religion? Well, the time is right, now that most people no longer attend church. For those souls who no longer give to a church yet fear that their current lifestyle might negatively influence their post-lifestyle, I thought up the name *Gateway to Heaven Fund*. In the good old pre-Reformation days, money was often a pre-condition for hobnobbing with the angels, and so it would be again.

I agonized over which of these funds to pursue and decided to pursue them both.

The fifty worst list taught me that the rules for creating and running a charity were, well, charitable. I was relieved to learn that 99.5% of charity applications were I.R.S. approved. We needn't go into form-filling details here, but the filings (or lack of filings) by the fifty worst gave me all the info I needed. Of course, if my enterprises were to be worthwhile, I did have to generate profit. And I did have to plan on how I was going to distribute circa 5% of those profits to the needy. After all, I am running a charity, you know.

In the 'what to distribute and how to expense categories,' the fifty worst again provided everything. Could I buy, say, air freshener at a sub-cost price, inflate its value, and distribute it to my charities? Yup. Could I inflate the shipping costs? Yup.

Now, all I have to do is raise the money and for that all I need is a telemarketing firm. When I was young, people wanted their kids to be doctors and lawyers. Today, we think a telemarketer in the family would be nice. And here comes the kicker. Not only is my daughter a telemarketer, she is marrying one. For their wedding present, I am giving them fifty percent of the money they generate from both new charities. Everybody's a winner. My daughter and future son-in-law win. The recipients who get the air freshener, or whatever, win. And the donors, who buy peace of mind, win big.

Do you need protection from the police? I'll send you a sticker for your car identifying you as a donor. Do you need to compensate for your transgressions? I'll send you a one-way ticket, guaranteed good, to you know where. You are all invited to donate to my funds. Let me know.

Everybody Wins

Why Do You Wear Clothes?

"Mommy, why do you wear clothes?"

"To stay warm."

"But it's warm in here."

"Well, hmmm, I like to wear clothes. Clothes are pretty."

"But, Mommy, you wear a robe when we are home. Mommy, is it because you want to hide your boobs?"

"Well, yes."

"Why?"

"Because they are private."

"But when you wear a swim-suit, your boobs mostly show."

"Johnny, don't you have homework?"

"Yes, Mommy, I'm doing it. The teacher told us to ask our mother or father a question and report our conversation to the class."

Be Careful What You Wish For

"Daddy, I want a dog."

"Get a robotic dog," I tell my kid.

"No, Daddy. I want a real dog."

"But think. You can play ball with a robo-dog. It can lick you. It can play ball. It can do all those things that a dog can do. And it won't poop in the house if you don't walk it. What's the problem?"

"It's not real."

"It *is* real! It's a real robo-dog."
"You can train it. You can train it to growl at bad guys and to pick up your toys."
"You can take it to robo-dog shows."
"You can give it presents at Christmas. What's not to like?"

"I want a real dog *and* a robo-dog. Then the robo-dog can play with the real dog when we are out."

"But the real dog might hurt the robo-dog. Why not get two robo-dogs that can play with each other while we're out and won't poop on the carpet if we don't get home on time. And don't get fleas. And don't go to the vet. And don't eat food or need water."

"But, sometimes robo-dogs need to get fixed."

"Fixed? Robo-dogs are gender neutral and *never* need fixing. That's another robo-dog plus."

"Even if it breaks?"

"Oh, I get it. Yes. If it breaks, we can get it fixed."

"Look, Kerry, do you love your dolls?"

"Yes."

"Do you love them full time?"

"Yes."

"Can you love a robo-dog?"

"Yes."

"What will you name your robo-dog?"

"I will name him Robo-dog."

"And what will you train Robo-dog to do?"

"Hmmmm. I think I will train Robo-dog to bark at you when you yell at Mommy. And I will train him to bite you when you drink too much. Daddy, when can I get my new robo-dog?"

Free Trials and Tribulations

How irresistible are these free trial offers that bombard us every day? Free delivery for just $5 a month. Automatic refills and get the first order free. Buy a subscription to Life-on-Mars Magazine and get 13 other magazines, no charge. You know the allure and the drill.

My mom has a lifetime supply of toothpaste with more coming every month. If she brushed her teeth every hour—instead of just once a week—she still couldn't use it up.

My uncle, who is now over 90, has 200 bottles of *Horny Goatweed Guaranteed Cure for Erectile Dysfunction* in his medicine chest—one of which was free. All of which are useless.

As for me, well, my free trials are bankrupting me. I can't keep track of what's on order or when to cancel it. My apartment looks like a landfill.

I now get hundreds of emails every day from hundreds of charities, addressed lovingly to dear Mickie. Some of these charities are real.

I have made it on to every sucker list. People who sell these lists to scammers are making a bundle off me. I should get a sucker cut.

At the urgent urging of all who stand to inherit my fortune, I decided to seek advice—free, online of course. And here's the advice I got on how to stop being a sucker—which I now pass on, free, to you:

1. Cancel your credit cards
2. Change your name
3. Move to the moon
4. Just stop being a sucker

Good luck.

Metrifying

The United States, along with the great nations of Liberia, Palau, and the Federated States of Micronesia defend the Imperial system of measures. All stand strong against the metric system. And we are the smarter for it. Yes! Because we imperial-system proponents get to count in increments of 12, as in 12 inches to a foot, whereas as others wimp out by using multiples of ten.

The metric system is just too easy. It breeds lazy minds.

Our politicians tried to wrest this ancient Babylonian system from us in the 1970s, but we have resisted. We want our water to boil at 212° instead of 100° as it does in the rest of the world and we want it to freeze at 32°, not at 0°.

Europeans *et al* measure distance in kilometers, with 1 kilometer equaling 1000 meters. Boring! We Americans travel in miles with one mile equaling 5,280 feet (or 1760 yards, if you prefer). Besides, what would we call Mile-High Stadium if we abandoned our system of miles? What would happen to common *clichés* like 'a miss is as good as a mile' (whatever that means)? Gone.

Now, people often argue against my stalwart anti-metric stance. Sometimes, they try to cajole me to change.

"Just think," they say, "On those roads now limited to sixty miles per hour, you could drive 100 kilometers an hour instead."

They insult me by saying that I defend a backward and confusing system because I am too stubborn to change my ways.

One detractor even argued that if evolution wanted us to use the Babylonian system it would have given us twelve fingers for counting, instead of the metric-ten fingers we have. But hey. That argument is as bogus as evolutionary theory itself.

So tell me you metric-maniacs. Just because your system is simple and sensible and universally used, why should this great nation adopt it?